Caillou

The Phone Call

Adaptation of the animated series: Marilyn Pleau-Murissi
Illustrations: Eric Sévigny, based on the animated series

"Mommy! Mommy!" Caillou said, tugging at her arm. But Mommy didn't answer. She was busy talking on the phone. She turned to Caillou, and said, "Caillou, I have work to do. Please give me a minute to get off the phone."

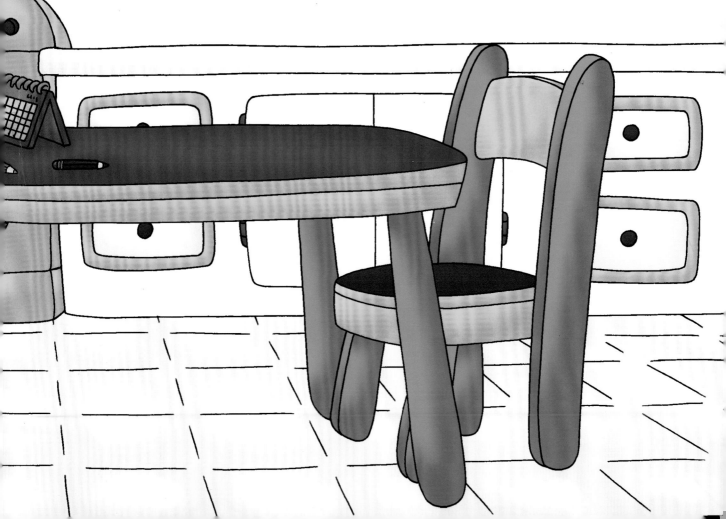

Caillou was sad. He had something important to tell her. Mommy hung up the phone and said, "I'm sorry, Caillou. Now what did you want to tell me?"
Caillou exclaimed, "It's Rosie! She tore up a book!"
The phone rang again and Mommy put up her hand. Caillou knew that meant he had to wait.

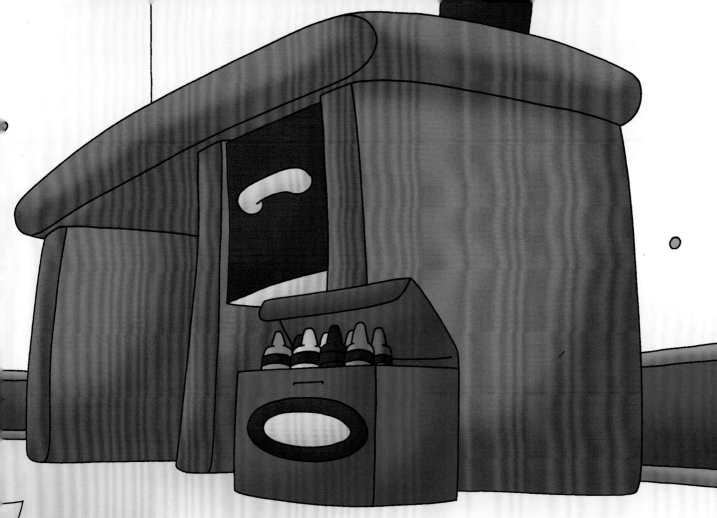

Caillou went to his room.

"I know, I'll draw Mommy a picture. She loves it when I draw for her," Caillou said.

When Caillou finished his picture, he was so excited he ran to the kitchen to bring it to Mommy.

"Look what I drew for you Mommy!" Caillou exclaimed.
Mommy was still on the phone.
When she hung up she said, "Let me see."
But the phone rang again.

"I'm sorry Caillou," Mommy said. "I know you've been waiting all morning. I'll be finished after this call." Caillou felt really bad. He felt like Mommy didn't care about him. He turned and walked away.

Caillou went to his room and looked around.
"I'll call Mommy on my phone," he said.
Just as he finished punching the numbers, the real phone rang.
"Wow!" Caillou said, surprised.

Caillou ran to the kitchen.
"Mommy that was me," he
said, watching her hang
up the phone.
Mommy smiled and began
to say, "No, Caillou, it..."
when the phone rang
again.
"Caillou, why don't you
answer that for me,"
Mommy said.

Caillou loved to
answer the phone.
It made him feel
grown-up.
"Hello!" he said.
"Grandma!... OK...
Mommy! Grandma
wants us to come
over. Can we?" he
asked.
"Sure," Mommy
answered. "Tell
Grandma we'll be
there soon."

"Caillou, do you remember this puppy?" Grandma asked as they walked in.

"Yes," Caillou answered, bending down to pet him.

"You can play with him. He would like that," Grandma said.

Caillou and Rosie were petting the puppy. He rolled over on his back, his paws in the air.

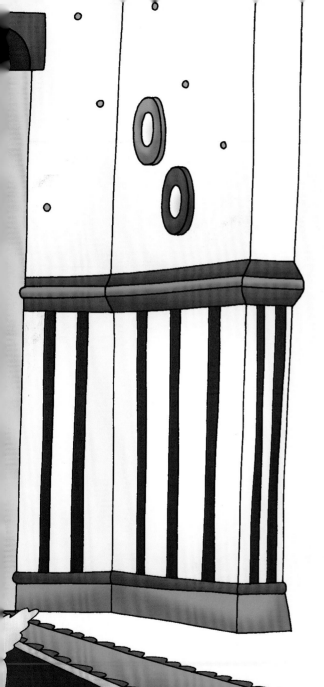

Suddenly the phone rang and the puppy jumped up barking. He ran over to Grandma and started tugging at her skirt. Caillou and Rosie were amazed.

Grandma hung up the phone and the puppy let go of her skirt. Caillou and Rosie started to laugh.

"Do you believe it?" Grandma said. "He does that every time I'm on the phone."

"Why?" Caillou asked.
"Maybe he thinks I'm
going to forget about
him," Grandma answered.
"Sounds like someone
I know," Mommy said,
smiling at Caillou.

Text: adaptation by Marilyn Pleau-Murissi of the animated series CAILLOU,
produced by DHX Media Inc.
All rights reserved.
Original story written by Matthew Cope.
Illustrations: Eric Sévigny, based on the animated series CAILLOU
Art Direction: Monique Dupras

The PBS KIDS logo is a registered mark of PBS and is used with permission.

We acknowledge the financial support of the Government of Canada through
the Canada Book Fund for our publishing activities.

Canadian Patrimoine
Heritage canadien

We acknowledge the support of the Ministry of Culture and Communications
of Quebec and SODEC for the publication and promotion of this book.
SODEC
Québec

National Library of Canada cataloguing in publication data

Pleau-Murissi, Marilyn
Caillou: the phone call
(Clubhouse)
For children aged 3 and up.

ISBN 978-2-89450-446-8

1. Telephone calls - Juvenile literature. 2. Oral communication -
Juvenile literature. I. CINAR Corporation. II. Title. III. Title: Phone
call. IV. Series.

P95.45.P53 2003   j302.3'46   C2003-940178-2

Printed in China
20 19 18 17 16 15 14 CHO1938 MAY2015